The Swan and the Crow
and
Other Folk-Tales

The Swan and the Crow
and
Other Folk-Tales

Collected by
W. CROOKE

Retold by
W. H. D. ROUSE

Illustrated by
W. H. ROBINSON

HAWK PRESS

Published by

Hawk Press
4836/24, Ansari Road, Daryaganj
New Delhi – 110 002
Phones : 9643330713, +91-11-23278618, +91-11-35676207
E-mail : thehawkpress@gmail.com
www.thehawkpress.com

Contents

Preface

THE stories contained in this little book are only a small part of a large collection of Indian folk-tales, made by Mr. Crooke in the course of the Ethnological Survey of the North-West Provinces and Oudh. Some were recorded by the collector from the lips of the jungle-folk of Mirzápur; others by his native assistant, Pandit Rámgharíb Chaubé. Besides these, a large number were received from all parts of the Provinces in response to a circular issued by Mr. J. C. Nesfield, the Director of Public Instruction, to all teachers of village schools.

The present selection is confined to the Beast Stories, which are particularly interesting as being mostly indigenous and little affected by so-called Aryan influence. Most of them are new, or have been published only in the *North Indian Notes and Queries*.

In the re-telling, for which Mr. Rouse is responsible, a number of changes have been made. The text of the book is meant for children, and consequently the first aim has been to make an interesting story. Those who study folk-tales for any scientific purpose will find all such changes marked in the Notes. If the change is considerable, the original document is summarised. It should be added that these documents are merely brief Notes in themselves, without literary interest. The Notes also give the source of each tale, and a few obvious parallels, or references to the literature of the subject.

The Swan and the Crow

Once upon a time, two Swans had to leave home on account of a famine; and they settled by a lake in a distant land. By the side of this lake lived a Carrion Crow. The Swans built a nest, and Mrs. Swan laid two beautiful round eggs in the nest, and sat upon them. She had to sit on the eggs for weeks, in order to keep them warm, so that the little ones might grow up inside and be hatched. While she sat there, the Crow used to help Mr. Swan to find food for his wife; and when the cygnets came out of their shells, the Crow helped to feed them also.

So all went happily for a time, and Mr. and Mrs. Swan were deeply grateful to the kind Crow. But Crows are not kind without some reason, and what this Crow's reason was, you shall now hear.

Time went on, and one day Mr. Swan said to Mrs. Swan--

"My dear, the famine must be over by this time. What do you say? shall we go home again?"

"I am ready," Mrs. Swan said, "and we can start to-morrow if you like."

"Stop a bit," says Mr. Crow, "I have a word or two to say first."

"Why, what do you mean?" the Swans said, both together.

"I mean," said the Crow, "that you may go, if you like, but these cygnets are as much mine as yours, and may I be plucked if I let them go with you!"

"Yours!" said Mrs. Swan. "Who laid the eggs? who hatched them?"

"And who fed them, I should like to ask?" said the Crow, with a disagreeable laugh: "Caw, caw, caw!"

Here was a bolt from the blue! The Crow stuck to it, and the end of all was, that Mrs. Swan stayed behind to look after her little ones, while Mr. Swan flew off to lay a complaint in court against the greedy Crow.

But you must not suppose that this Crow meant to sit still, and let the Swan have things all his own way. Not he; off he flew secretly to the Judge, and to the Judge said he--

"O Judge, a Swan is going to lodge a false charge against me, and I want your help!"

"If it is false," said the Judge, "you want help from no one."

"Caw, caw, caw!" said the Crow, "you understand me." Then this vulgar Crow winked one eye at the Judge.

"Hm, hm," said the Judge, looking at the Crow. It is a pity to say it, but it is quite true, that this Judge was an unjust Judge; and he was ready to give any decision, right or wrong, so long as he was bribed well for his trouble. In that country, you see, there was no jury to decide matters, but all power lay in the hands of the Judge.

The Judge winked one eye at the Crow. Then he said, very softly, "~What will you give me?~"

"Silver and gold have I none," said the Crow, "but I'll tell you what I will do. I'll carry your father's bones to the Holy Land, and bury them in Jerusalem, and then your father will be sure to go to heaven."

The Judge was so foolish that he really believed his father would go to heaven at once, if only his bones were buried in Jerusalem, although his father had been as wicked as himself while he was alive. So he agreed to the Crow's proposal.

When the case came into court, of course the Judge gave decision in favour of the Crow, though there was no evidence on his side except his own word: and who but a fool would trust the word of a Carrion Crow? When the court rose, the Crow flew to the house of the Judge, and asked for the bones of the Judge's father. So the Judge tied up his father's bones in a bag, and hung the bag round the Crow's neck. Away flew the Crow, but he didn't fly far; for as the Judge watched him, the Crow hovered over a filthy drain; and untying the bag, began dropping the bones one by one into the mud.

"Hi, you brute!" shouted the Judge, "what are you doing!"

"Oh, you pumpkin!" said the Crow, "did you verily think that I should take the trouble to carry your father's rotten old bones to Jerusalem? No, no; I only wanted to see what rogues the race of Judges can be.
Caw!" Flop! went the last bone into the mud, and away flew the Crow, and never came back there any more.

So the Judge had to pick his father's bones out of the gutter. And the next thing he had to do was to reverse his own decision, and give the Swan his young ones again; because, you see, a great many people had heard what the Crow said to the Judge, and knew (if they didn't know it before) that the Judge was a rogue. So the Swan got his young ones back, and as for the Judge, he became the laughing-stock of the whole city, and he was obliged to go and try his tricks elsewhere.

Pride shall Have a Fall

There was once a great drought in the land. For weeks and months not a drop of rain fell; and the sun beat down, and dried up the whole country, so that there was no water to be found. Now there was a certain pond in that country; and as day after day the sun blazed, the water sank lower and lower, until it was hardly an inch deep. Numbers of Frogs used to live in this pond; but as the water dried the Frogs died, so that the dry mud on the banks of the pond was covered all over with dead bodies of Frogs.

There came a Jackal out of the forest. He was glad to see this pool, because the pool where he used to drink had been quite dried up. So he made a little platform of mud, and stuck up four posts at the four corners; and then he gathered bundles of dry grass, and put them upon the top of the four posts for a thatch. Then his eye fell on the corpses of Frogs lying about; and being a foolish animal, he thought these corpses were uncommonly pretty. And what do you think he did? He
gathered a lot of the dead Frogs and hung a fringe of them all round the thatch; and in each of his ears he hung a dead Frog, like an earring.

From far and near swarms of Rats used to come to this pond for drinking, since it was the only water to be found for a long distance, and all the rest was dried up. Then the Jackal kept guard over the pool; and not a drop might any Rat so much as taste, unless he would first bow down and worship the Jackal, and sing the following psalm, which the Jackal made up himself:--

> "A temple all of gold I found,
> With golden lamps hung all around;
> And see! the God himself is here,
> With two big pearls in either ear."

Even a Rat can tell a dead Frog from a pearl, but willy nilly he needs must sing it, or else no water. So when the Rat had sung this psalm, and bowed himself down three times before the Jackal, worshipping him as if he were a God, he was allowed to go down and take a sip of the water.

One day, what should come down to the water to drink but an Ox with one eye.

"Ho! ho! one-eyed Ox!" screamed the Jackal, "not a drop till you sing your psalm."

The Ox blinked his one eye stupidly, and looked round. "What psalm?" asked the one-eyed Ox.

"Mine," said the Jackal, who was very proud of his psalm, "my own composition." Then he sang it over to the Ox, that he might hear it.

"'A temple all of gold I found--'

"That's this, you know," he explained, pointing to the scraggy thatch--

> "A temple all of gold I found,
> With golden lamps hung all around;
> And see! the God himself is here,
> With two big pearls in either ear."

"Ah," said the one-eyed Ox, "I'm rather stupid, I fear, and it will take me a minute or two to learn that psalm. It's a mighty fine psalm, that; I never heard the like in church. Suppose I say it over to myself while I'm a-drinking? that will save time, and it would be a thousand pities to spoil a thing like that."

This flattered the Jackal so much that he agreed.

One-eye went down to the pool, and took a long, long pull at the water. Then he came out of the water, and went slowly up to the Jackal, as he was sitting under his thatch, with its string of dead Frogs, and the two
Frogs in the Jackal's ears.

"Now then, booby!" the Jackal said, "look sharp, the God is waiting."

The Ox opened a big mouth, and in a very hoarse voice he sang--

> "A nasty dirty thatch I found,
> With dried-up Frogs hung all around;
> And see! the mangy Jackal here,

With two dead Frogs in either ear."

You may imagine the rage of the Jackal to hear this! He fairly foamed at the mouth. "You blasphemous beast!" screamed he, "I'll teach you to abuse a God!" And with that he jumped down off his seat, and gave chase.

Away scuttled the Ox; and as he ran, the water he had been drinking went gurgling inside him, flippity-flop, flippity-flop.

This sound rather frightened the Jackal. "What's that?" he cried.

"A dog at your heels," said the Ox.

The Jackal was so scared at the very name of dog, that he turned about in no time, blind with terror, and away he scampered as hard as he could pelt. He was so frightened, that he did not see where he was going; so he ran straight into the midst of a pack of hounds, who made short work of the conceited Jackal.

The Kid and the Tiger

A Nanny-Goat and a Tigress were near neighbours in a certain wood, and fast friends to boot. The Tigress had two tiger-cubs; and the family of the Nanny-goat were four frolicksome kids, named Roley, Poley, Skipster, and Jumpster.

But the Tigress was jealous of her friend the Nanny-goat, because Nanny had four young ones, while she had only two. One day, as she was musing on the injustice of her fate, she thought to herself, "What if I eat up two of Nanny's kids, and then things will be equal? They do say, friends have all things in common." So to Nanny-goat she hied, and said she--

"Sister Nanny, my little ones have gone out, and I am very lonely at home. Do let one of your dear kiddies come and sleep with me, for company. Will you, please?"

"Gladly will I, sister," said honest Nanny-goat, thinking no evil of her friend. Then she ran out to the fields, where Roley and

Poley were rolling over each other, and Jumpster was jumping over the back of Skipster.

"Children, children!" said Nanny-goat, "a treat for you! A kind friend has asked one of you out to spend the night."

"Baa baa baa!" cried the Kids, running up; and then three of them called out all together, dancing about old Nanny, "Let me go! Let me go! Let me go!" But the fourth, who was a wise little imp (and Roley it was, to be sure), asked in a quiet tone, "Who is it, Mammy Nanny-goat?"

"Why, who should it be but your Aunt Yellowstripe?" said Nanny.

At this they all looked rather crestfallen; for although Nanny-goat loved her friend dearly, all the youngsters were afraid of her, for what reason they could not say. Children have a way of finding out their friends; and these Kids had noticed at times a gleam in the eyes of Auntie Yellowstripe, which boded ill to little Kids.

"No-o, thank you, Mammy Nanny-goat," said Skipster, skipping away.

"No-o-o, thank you, Mammy," said Jumpster, and jumped after her.

"No-o-o-o, thank you," said Poley, and rolled away by himself.

Why did Poley roll away by himself? Because Roley stayed behind. Roley did not say No, thank you; on the contrary, he said Yes. Why Roley said yes instead of no, was his own concern; and I think Roley knew what he was about.

This was how Roley went with the Tigress; and that night the Tigress put him to sleep by her side. She cuddled him up, and made a great fuss of him, thinking to herself, "Soft words cost nothing; and when he is fast asleep, we shall see what we shall see."

But Roley was no such fool as the Tigress thought him. So he did not go to sleep, but only pretended; and no sooner did Dame Yellowstripe begin to snore, than up jumps Roley, as soft as you please, and fetches out one of Yellowstripe's own cubs, who were sleeping away at the back of the cave. He laid the cub in his own place, and went into the corner to sleep with the other cub.

About midnight the Tigress awoke, and as she felt the warm little thing nestling beside her, she chuckled to herself. Then she gave him one tap with her mighty paw; crack! went his neck, and his dancing days were over; the Tigress gobbled him up, skin, bones, and teeth. It was pitch dark, you know, and she could not see that she was eating her own cub. "One less of the brood now," thought the Tigress; turned over, and went to sleep again.

Next morning, they all woke up; and Yellowstripe, to her dismay, saw that Roley was rolling about, right as a trivet. She looked round for her own cubs, and lo and behold! one was missing. At first she could not make it out in the least; but when it dawned upon her what had happened, she nearly turned yellow all over with rage and disappointment.

"Did you have a good night, Roley dear?" said she in a wheedling tone to the Kid.

"Oh yes, Auntie," said the little Kid, "only a gnat bit me."

This astonished the Tigress, who thought that the Kid must be stronger than he appeared to be. "Never mind," said she to herself; "come to-night, we shall see what we shall see."

That night all went as before; only this time Roley put a huge stone in his place, and then he ran off as fast as his legs could carry him. When the Tigress awoke, she gave a pat to the stone: it hurt her paw sadly.

"Good heavens," said she, "what a mighty Kid it is, to be sure! I must make short work of him now I have the chance, or there is no knowing what may happen. When he grows up, he may kill me." So she gave a fierce bite at the stone, and broke all her front teeth.

Now the Tigress' fury knew no bounds. She went raging about the cave, hunting in every corner for Roley; but Roley was not to be found, because, as I have told you, he was not there. So the Tigress was forced to wait until morning for her revenge.

All night long the Tigress lay awake with the pain of her teeth; and when morning came, she sought out a familiar friend to take counsel with. This friend was an old one-eyed Tiger. The Tigress and the one-eyed Tiger talked for a long time together, and as they talked they walked. When they came to the end of their talk, their walk was also at an end, and they found themselves at the mouth of Yellowstripe's den.

There in the den, as calm as you please, playing with the one remaining Tiger cub, was Roley.

"Ha ha," laughed One-eye, "so there you are. Let us sit down, and I will tell you a story."

"Do, do, Nuncle One-eye," cried Roley.

So they all sat down, and One-eye began. "When I eat little Kids," said One-eye, "four of them make me a mouthful; and I'm coming one of these days to make one mouthful of you and your brother and sisters."

"Capital, capital, Nuncle One-eye!" said Roley, clapping his paws; "what good stories you do tell, Nuncle One-eye! Now I'll tell you a story. When you come to eat us up, Skipster will hold you by the forelegs, and Jumpster will hold you by the hind legs, and Poley will hold your head, and Roley will chop it off, if only mother will give us a light."

This terrified One-eye extremely, for he was a great coward. He thought it all as true as gospel, so he took to his heels, and left Yellowstripe in the lurch.

On the way, he met six other Tigers, friends of his. "Oh my friends!" said he, "I have such a treat for you! A fine fat Kid, crying out to be killed! Come along, come along, I'll show you the way, and all I ask is the pleasure of serving you." Cunning old One-eye!

The six Tigers believed all that One-eye said, and away they all trotted together towards the place where Roley lived. They knew he would go home sooner or later; and indeed he was there already, and saw them coming, so he climbed up a tree. Goats are wonderfully good at climbing rocks, but I think most of them cannot climb trees; still, whatever may be true of other goats, Roley could. If it were not so, this story would never have been written. So Roley climbed up a tree, and sat on a branch, with his legs all dangling in the air.

The first Tiger gave a jump, and missed him. Number two gave a jump, and missed him. They all jumped, one after another, and not one of them could touch Roley; who sat and laughed at them so heartily, that he nearly fell off his perch.

At last, when they were tired of jumping, and jumping, up gets old One-eye, and says, "I know how to get at him. I'll stand here, and you get on my back, and then the rest of you one a-top of another, and then we shall catch him nicely." They all thought this an excellent idea; so One-eye propped his old carcass against the tree, and the other Tigers mounted one on another's shoulders, until there they were, all seven in a pyramid. Then the topmost Tiger stretched out his paw, and all but got hold of Roley.

Thereupon One-eye cocked up his solitary eye, to see how things were going on up aloft; and seeing this, Roley called out--

"Mother, give me a lump of mud, and I'll hit the brute in his sound eye, and then we will finish him off."

When One-eye heard this, he gave a great start, and down toppled the whole seven in a heap, one a-top of the next, spitting and roaring and scratching. They were so much taken aback, that they imagined all sorts of powerful beasts to be fighting with them, when it was only their own selves, biting each other; and the end of all was, that as soon as the seven Tigers had each got his four legs to himself, off they went helter-skelter into the forest, and never more troubled Mammy Nanny-goat and her four frolicsome Kids.

The Stag, the Crow, and the Jackal

Once upon a time there was a Stag living in a certain jungle, and in the same jungle lived a Crow. These two were bosom friends. Why a Stag should take a fancy to a Crow, I cannot say; but so it was; and if you do not believe it, you had better not read any further.

It so befell that a Jackal came by one day, and his eye fell on this Stag, and a fine plump Stag he was. The Jackal's mouth began to water. How he would like to make a meal of so dainty a piece of flesh. But he knew it was of no use trying to attack the Stag, who seemed very strong. Still, by hook or by crook, that Stag he would have. So in the depths of his cunning heart he concocted a trick, of which you shall shortly hear.

The Jackal watched his chance, and as soon as he had found the Stag alone, he began to say, sidling up to the Stag, and whispering in his ear--

"Beware of that Crow; he's fooling thee. Beware, beware all birds of the air. There's no trusting any bird, let alone a Crow, who is worst of the whole feathered tribe. Now you and I, who never try in the air to fly, good honest gentlemen with four legs apiece, we are marked out for friends by Nature herself."

Will you be surprised to hear that the Stag listened to the crafty and slanderous words, and deserted his friend the Crow? When your hair is grey you will know that such is the way of the world, and that a true friend who sticks to the end, is harder to find than a diamond mine.

But although this Stag was shallow-hearted and weak, not so the Crow. He was a true friend, and he was cut to the heart by the unkindness of his friend the Stag; but he wasted no time in fruitless tears. He went about his work as usual, and waited for a chance of winning back his recreant friend.

Well, Stag and Jackal scoured about the woods together, and the Jackal did his best to make himself agreeable. In this he had poor success; for though the Stag tried hard to like his new comrade, yet he could not help seeing that he was dirty; moreover, the Jackal ate all sorts of dead animals, but the Stag was a vegetarian, and did not approve of this kind of food.

But though the Stag had qualms now and again, he was not strong enough to break loose from the friendship of the Jackal.

But the time was ripening for the Jackal's blow. He knew a place where huntsmen used to set gins and snares, to catch the wild animals. So one day, as he and the Stag were out a-walking together, the Jackal so managed that they passed by this place.

The Jackal took good care to keep clear of the snare; but the innocent Stag knew nothing of snares or gins, so into a snare he stept, and snap! he was fast.

Now was the time for a true friend to show his friendship. But the Jackal, as we already know, was a humbug; accordingly, all he did was to sit by the side of the Stag, and try not to look pleased.

"Oh dear, what shall I do?" said the Stag, when he found himself caught. "Oh my friend, do help me out."

"You shock me, friend," said the Jackal, pulling a long face; "surely you have not forgotten that it is Sunday? We are told in the Ten Commandments to do no work on the Sabbath day. If it were not so, how gladly would I help you!" So saying, he wiped away a crocodile tear.

He sat down and waited in the hope that the Stag would die, and then he would eat him.

But the faithful Crow was not far. Though his friend the Stag would not so much as cast him a look, the Crow followed him ever, biding his time; and now the time had come.

The Crow perched on a neighbouring tree, and said--

"Dear friend, I am only a weak little bird, and I cannot help you; but I can teach you to help yourself. My advice is, pretend to be dead, and when the Hunter comes, he will open the snare without any care, and you can escape."

"Thank you, long-suffering friend!" said the Stag; and so he did. When the Huntsman came, he thought the Stag was dead; he opened the snare, and before he was aware, the Stag was up and off and away.

The Stag asked his friend the Crow to forgive him, and they lived happily together as before. As for the treacherous Jackal, he never came near them more.

The Monkey and the Crows

On a certain land, a flock of Crows built their nests in the branches of a huge cotton-tree.

In that country, the climate is not the least like ours. It is hot all the year round, and for eight months the sun blazes like a fiery furnace, so that the people who live there are burnt as black as your boot; then after eight months comes the rain, and the rain comes down in bucketsful, with lightning fit to blind you, and thunder enough to crack your head. These Crows were quite happy in their nests, whatever happened; for when it was hot, the leaves of the trees sheltered them from the sun, and in the rainy season the leaves kept them pretty dry.

One evening there came a terrible storm, with torrents of rain like Noah's flood. In the midst of it, the Crows noticed a Monkey sliding along, drenched and draggle-tailed, looking like a drowned Rat. The Crows set up a chorus of caws, and called out--

"O Monkey, what a fool you must be! Look at us, dry and comfortable, in our nests of rags and twigs. If we, with only our little beaks to help us, can make comfortable nests, why can't you, with two hands and two feet and a tail?"

You might have thought the Monkey would take this advice to heart. But not a bit of it. Monkeys are naturally a lazy tribe, and they are full of envy, hatred, and malice. What they like best is destroying whatever they can lay their hands on; and when I look upon some of the nations of this globe, I cannot help thinking that they really must be descended from Monkeys. So this Monkey snapt and snarled, and said to the Crows--

"Just wait till morning, and then we'll see what a Monkey can do."

The simple birds were delighted to hear this, and looked forward to seeing the Monkey do something wonderfully clever, with his tail and his two hands and two feet.

Morning came, and the rain was over. The Monkey climbed up into the tree, and in his rage and envy he tore all the Crows' nests to pieces.

Then the Crows were sorry they spoke, and determined for the future to mind their own business, and let fools alone. For, as the wise man said, "To give good advice to a fool is like pouring oil upon the fire."

The Swan and the Paddy-Bird

A wild Swan was flying once to his home, when he paused to rest on a tree. This was a kind of tree you have most likely never seen. It was very tall, and had no branches upon it until you came to the top, but at the top was a large clump of green leaves, and bunches of cocoa-nuts hanging down.

It so happened that on this tree was the nest of a Paddy-bird. A Paddy-bird is a bird something like a heron, which feeds on fish and frogs. At the moment when the Swan perched upon the tree, this Paddy-bird was sitting demurely on the edge of a pond that was below the tree, watching the water for a rise. She had no fishing-rod, but when she saw a little fish or a frog swim past, out went her beak like a flash, and the fish was pierced. Then she ate the fish, or carried it off to her little ones in the nest.

When the Paddy-bird chanced to look round, she saw the Swan sitting upon her tree. She was frightened at this, thinking that perhaps it was some bird of prey, come to devour her chicks. So she left her fishing, and at once flew up to the top of the cocoa-nut tree. The Swan looked harmless enough when she came closer, so plucking up courage, the Paddy-bird thus addressed him--

"Good-day, sir. May I ask who you are?"

"I am a Swan," said the other, "and I am on my way home; but as it is a hot day, I thought I would rest awhile on your tree. I hope you have no objection?"

"Welcome, my lord Swan, welcome!" said the Paddy-bird. "I only wish I could offer you entertainment. But I am ashamed to say that I have no food worth your taking. I am a poor bird, and you know we Paddy-birds eat only small fish and frogs, which your highness would hardly touch."

"Oh, never mind for that," answered the Swan; "thank you all the same, but I can find my own food on this tree of yours."

This set our Paddy-bird's heart all a-flutter, for what could he mean but her brood? However, all was well in a minute; when she saw the Swan go to one of the green cocoa-nuts hanging to the tree. You have seen, I suppose, three little soft places at the top of a cocoa-nut, which are holes in the shell filled up with pulp. The Swan pierced his bill through one of these holes, and drank the milk inside the cocoa-nut. Then he gave some of the milk to the Paddy-bird, and flew away.

This milk tasted very nice, and the Paddy-bird began to say to herself, "What a fool I have been all these years! Here am I, watching and waiting all day long for a frog, and nasty things they are too, and all this while there was plenty of delicious milk within a yard of my nest! Well, good-bye fish, and good-bye frogs; I have done with you now for ever."

The next time the Paddy-bird felt hungry, she flew to a cocoa-nut and began to peck at it. But she did not know the secret of the three little holes at the top of the cocoa-nut; so she pecked, and pecked, and got no further. At last she gathered all her strength, and gave a tremendous peck at the cocoa-nut. Snap! her bill broke off, and the blood ran out, and very soon the poor Paddy-bird had bled to death.

Next day, the Swan happened to fly by that way again; and coming to the tree, he found his friend the Paddy-bird lying dead on the ground, with her bill snapt off clean. He understood at once what had happened, and said to himself, "This is what comes of trying to do what one is not fit for. Let the cobbler stick to his last, or misfortune follows fast."

What is a Man ?

On a certain forest, a Lioness dwelt who had one cub. This cub did not go to school, as you one day will go; but he learned his lessons at home. And what do you think his lessons were? Not multiplication which is vexation; not the Rule of Three which puzzles me; not spelling and copy-books. No; the Lioness had only one lesson to teach her cub, and that was, to avoid mankind as if they were poison. Every day, morning and evening, she taught him for an hour; telling him again and again, that of all the beasts of the forest he need fear none, for a lion is stronger than any, but man he must fear and keep clear of.

Well, the little Lion grew big; and as often happens to children as well as lions' cubs, he grew conceited too. He could not believe that his mother was old enough to know better than he; no, he would see for himself. So one fine day, this Lion set out on a voyage of discovery.

The first thing he saw was an Ox. This Ox was a fine sturdy animal, and the Lion felt rather nervous to see such hoofs and horns. You must remember he was young and ignorant, and had hardly seen any animal but his mother and father. So he went up to the Ox, and said timidly--

"Good morning, sir. Will you be good enough to tell me if you are a Man?"

If an Ox could laugh, that Ox would have laughed in the face of the Lion's cub. But an Ox is always solemn, like a Turk, though he does not love bloodshed as a Turk does. This Ox was chewing the cud, munching and mouthing with great calmness, so as to get the full flavour of the rich grass. He turned his meek eyes, and stared at the Lion. Then he said--

"A Man! God forbid. A Man is a terrible creature. He makes slaves of us Oxen, and puts a yoke on our necks and fastens us to a thing called a plough; and makes us pull the plough to and fro, up and down, till we are tired to death. If we won't go, he sticks a prod into us, which hurts us very much. I can't think what is the use of all this pother; we get no good of it. And when we are old, and can work no more, he kills us, and eats our flesh, and the skin he makes into shoes for his own feet. Keep clear of Men, if you value your life." Then the Ox turned his head away, and went on with his chewing.

This gave our Lion something to think about. He thought the Ox a very fine animal indeed, and yet, said the Ox, Man was stronger.

The Lion went his ways, and by-and-by, what should he see but a Camel. If the Ox was a fine creature, here was a finer; ever so tall, with a hump on his back, and a long neck, and great long legs. Surely this must be the terrible Man he had heard so much of. But to make certain, he approached the Camel with great respect, and said--

"Good morning, sir. Pray, will you tell me if you are a Man?"

The Camel turned his long neck, and sniffed and sneered as Camels have a way of doing, and a most unpleasant way it is.

"Pooh!" said he. "Stuff! poof! you oaf! you think me a Man? I wish I were a Man, wouldn't I make short work of you! A man, quotha! Why, I am a slave to that same Man. They catch us, these Men, and make a hole in our noses, and put a ring in it--do you see my ring? How do you think I like a hole made in my nose, as if two holes were not enough! Then they tie a rope to the ring, and lead us about all day long just where they please, without a with your leave, or by your leave! And they make us squat down in the mud, and put a great load on our backs, enough to crush a whipper-snapper like you. Groan as we may, it's all of no use, they do what they choose. Man! the very name makes me shiver. Get out, and leave me alone!"

This frightened our Lion, because who knew whether the great animal might not kill him, if it came into his head, so the Lion went away as fast as he could.

In a little while, he espied an Elephant. Here was a monster, to be sure! A great black mountain, with a long nose curling about, and huge white teeth sticking out, and big ears flapping. The Lion was quite terrified this time, and would not go near the Elephant, until he suddenly saw that the Elephant had a rope round his tusks, by which he was tied fast to a stake. Then he plucked up courage to approach, and said--

"Good morning, my lord. Please will you tell me, are you a Man?"

The Elephant trumpeted loudly. That was his way of laughing at the idea that he could be mistaken for a Man.

"Hooroo! hooroo!" he shrieked. "A Man! Hooroo! No, but a Man is my master, and that's the truth. A Man tied me to this post. Cruel and selfish brutes, are men; and with all my strength, I am no match for a Man. They get on our backs, a dozen of them at a time, and make us fetch, and carry, and drive us about by sticking a sharp spike into our skulls. Don't you go near a Man, if you love your life; why, bless me, they will make mincemeat of you! Hooroo!" The Elephant swished his trunk all round him in his excitement.

Our Lion had now seen three astonishing creatures, and they all said that a Man was stronger than they were. What could this terrible creature be like? He must be a mountain indeed, if he was to master such a beast as the black Elephant. Yet the black creature said that Men got on his back, a dozen of them at a time. The Lion could not understand it at all. He shook his head, and stalked away thoughtful.

As the Lion was going along, he saw a puny and weak-looking thing, walking upright on two legs. He seemed to be a kind of monkey, thought the Lion. It never entered his head that this little thing could be a Man, but he trotted up to him gaily, and said--

"Good morning, my friend. Can you tell me where I can find a Man? I have been hunting for one all the morning."

"I am a Man," said the other.

At this the Lion laughed in his face. "You a Man!" said he. "Come, come; I may be young, but I am no fool, my good fellow. Why, you are not so big as one leg of that mountain over there, who was tied to a stake, as he said, by a Man."

"All the same," the Man said, "I am one of them."

"But look here," the Lion went on, "my father and mother both say that Man is a terrible and cruel creature, and the only creature a Lion need fear. Now, either you are no Man, or else my father and mother are quite wrong."

"Well," said the Man, "I am not nearly so strong as you are, or the Elephant and Camel, or even the Ox. As you say, I am not much to look at, but I have one power which you all lack."

"Indeed," said the Lion, "and what may that be?"

The Man answered, "Reason."

"I never heard of reason," said the Lion. "Please explain it to me, will you?"

"It is not easy to explain what reason is," replied the Man; "but if you like, I will show you how it works."

The Lion was pleased. "Oh please do," he said.

I must tell you that this Man was a woodcutter, and he had an axe upon his shoulder. He now lifted this axe and drove a blow into a stout sapling which grew hard by. When he had split the sapling, he took a wedge of wood, and hammered it in with the back of his axe, until there was a large cleft in the trunk of the sapling.

"Now then," said the Man,
"just put your paw in that hole."

The Lion obediently put his paw into the cleft, and then the Man pulled out the wedge from the cleft. The sapling closed tight on the paw of the Lion, and squeezed it. "Now," said the Man, "you know what reason is."

But the Lion no longer cared to hear about reason; all he wanted was to get his paw out of the cleft. He pulled and he tugged, he roared and he struggled; but all of no use; he could not by any means get his paw free. The end of all was, in madness and fury he dashed his head against the ground, and died.

This was how the Lion learnt how terrible a being is Man; but unluckily, you see, his knowledge was of no use to him or any one else, because it cost him his life. If he had listened to his mother's teaching, he might be living still, and you would not be reading this story.

The Wound and the Scar

There a certain forest, a Lioness dwelt who had one cub. This cub did not go to school, as you one day will go; but he learned his lessons at home. And what do you think his lessons were? Not multiplication which is vexation; not the Rule of Three which puzzles me; not spelling and copybooks. No; the Lioness had only one lesson to teach her cub, and that was, to avoid mankind as if they were poison. Every day, morning and evening, she taught him for an hour; telling him again and again, that of all the beasts of the forest he need fear none, for a lion is stronger than any, but man he must fear and keep clear of.

was once a forest where a Lion dwelt. Over all the beasts of the forest the Lion lorded it, and of men not one durst come near the place for fear of King Lion; none, that is, except one only, a Woodman who lived in a little hut just upon the borders of the woodland; and between the forest and the hut a river flowed. This Woodman came often into the forest, to cut wood; and he had no fear to do so, because the Lion and he were bosom friends. Such fast friends they were that if ever the Woodman failed to pay his daily visit, the Lion was grieved and missed him sorely.

It happened once that the Woodman fell ill of a fever. In his woodland hut he lay all alone, for no wife was there, or sister to care for him. So he tossed and moaned, and waited for the hours to pass.

Of course during all this time the Woodman could not visit the forest, and his friend the Lion missed him. "What can be the matter," thought King Lion. "Has some enemy killed him, or has he fallen sick?" At last he could no longer bear the suspense, and set out in search of the Woodman.

I do not think that the Lion had ever yet been to his friend's house; and for all he knew he might be walking straight into a trap. But he was so fond of the Woodman that he never thought of danger. All he wanted was to see his friend. Accordingly, he followed the path by which the Woodman came into the woods; and in due time this path led him to the bank of a wide and swift river, and over on the opposite bank was a hut.

In plunged the Lion, not waiting to think; and though there were crocodiles in that river ready to eat him, and though the current bade fair to sweep him away, so strong was his love for his friend that he swam across.

The Woodman's house stood within an enclosure, and all the doors and gates were shut; but the Lion jumped over the wall, and searched about, until he managed somehow to force his way into the house. Then he saw his friend lying upon a bed, and very ill, all alone, with no one to tend him.

How grieved the Lion was to see his friend, you can imagine better than I can tell. The Lion knelt down by his friend's side, and began to lick him all over. This woke the man from his dazed condition; and when he found the Lion licking his body, he did not like the smell of the Lion, so he turned his head away, with a grunt of disgust.

Now I think this was very unkind, because the Lion had no other way of showing how much he cared for his friend. Think what a long way he had come to see his friend, and think what danger he had faced; and now to be met with a grunt of disgust! The Lion stopped licking the Woodman, and got up slowly, and went away. Back he swam over the deep and swift river, but all the heart was taken out of him; he cared not for the crocodiles, indeed now he would not have been very sorry if a crocodile had devoured him.

One crocodile did actually get a nip at his leg, and left a wound there. Back to his den he crept, solitary and sad. And when he got to his den, he lay down, sick of his friend's fever, which he had taken by licking him.

In a week or so, the Woodman was well again; and thinking nothing of what had passed, he shouldered his axe, and trudged away to cut wood.

When the time came for his midday meal, he went as his custom was to the Lion's den; and there he found his friend the Lion, thin and sick.

"Why, friend, what is the matter?" the Woodman asked.

"I am ill," said the Lion.

"What is it?" asked the Woodman again.

But the Lion would answer nothing; and do what he would, the man could not get him to say another word. So he left him for that day, and went home.

For several days after, the man did the same thing; and gradually the Lion got better.

At last one day, when the Lion was quite well again, the man said to him--

"Tell me, good friend Lion, what it is that has made you so silent and gloomy of late?"

Then answered the Lion, "O Woodman, I will tell you. When you were ill, I swam a swift river and faced death, all for your sake; I came into your house when you lay deserted, and licked your body, and took the fever which you had into my veins; and this wound which you see, I received from a crocodile as I was swimming across on my way back. But you received me with scorn, and turned away your face in disgust.

The fever is gone, and this wound (as you see) is healed; but the wound in my heart can never heal. You are no true friend; and from henceforth our ways lie apart."

The man was ashamed of his unkindness, but it was too late, for, as the poet says--

"Who snaps the thread of friendship, never more Can join it as it once was joined before."

The Cat and the Parrot

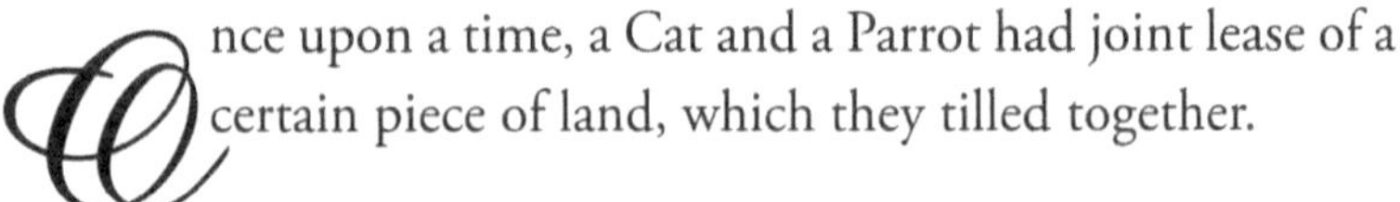

Once upon a time, a Cat and a Parrot had joint lease of a certain piece of land, which they tilled together.

One day the Cat said to the Parrot, "Come, friend, let us go to the field."

Said the Parrot, "I can't come now, because I am whetting my bill on the branch of a mango-tree."

So the Cat went alone, and ploughed the field. When the field was ploughed, the Cat came to the Parrot again, and said--

"Come, friend, let us sow the corn."

Said the Parrot, "I can't come now, because I am whetting my beak on the branch of a mango-tree."

So the Cat went alone, and sowed the corn. The corn took root, the corn sprouted, it put forth the blade, and the ear, and the ripe corn in the ear. Then again the Cat came to the Parrot, and said--
"Come, friend, let us go and gather the harvest."

Said the Parrot, "I can't come now, because I am whetting my beak on the branch of a mango-tree."

So the Cat went alone, and gathered the harvest. She put it away in barns, and made ready for threshing. When all was ready for the threshing, again the Cat came to the Parrot, and said--

"Come, friend, let us thresh the corn."

Said the Parrot, "I can't come now, because I am whetting my beak on the branch of a mango-tree."

So the Cat went, and threshed all the corn alone. Then the Cat came back to the Parrot, and said--

"Come, friend, let us go and winnow the grain from the chaff."

Said the Parrot, "I can't come now, because I am whetting my beak on the branch of a mango-tree."

So the Cat winnowed the grain from the chaff alone. Then she came back once again to the Parrot, and said--

"Come, friend, the grain is all winnowed and sifted; come and divide it between us."

"Certainly," said the Parrot, and came at once. You see the Cat had done all the work, but the Parrot was quite ready to share the profit. They divided the corn into two halves, and the Cat put her half away somewhere, and the Parrot carried his half to his nest.

Then the Cat and the Parrot agreed to invite each other to dinner every day; that is to say, the Cat asks the Parrot to-day, and the Parrot asks the Cat to-morrow. The Cat's turn came first. Then the Cat went to market and bought a ha'porth of milk, a ha'porth of sugar, and a ha'porth of rice. When the Parrot came there was nothing but this stingy fare. Moreover, the Cat was so inhospitable, that she actually made the Parrot cook the food himself! Perhaps that was her way of rebuking her friend for his laziness.

Next day the turn came to the Parrot. He procured about thirty pounds of flour, and plenty of butter, and everything else that was needed, and cooked the food before his guest came. He made enough cakes to fill a washerwoman's basket--about five hundred.

When the Cat came, the Parrot put before her four hundred and ninety-eight cakes, in a heap, and kept back for himself only two. The Cat ate up the four hundred and ninety-eight cakes in about three minutes, and then asked for more.

The Parrot set before her the two cakes he had kept for himself. The Cat devoured them, and then asked for more.

The Parrot said, "I have no more cakes, but if you are still hungry, you may eat me."

The Cat was still hungry, and ate the Parrot, bones and beak and feathers. Thus the tables were turned; for if the Parrot had the best of it before, the Cat had the best of it now.

An old woman happened to be near, and saw this. So she picked up a stone, and said--

"Shoo! shoo! get away, or I'll kill you with this stone."

Now the Cat thought to herself, "I ate a basketful of cakes, I ate my friend the Parrot, and shall I blush to eat this old hag?"

No, surely not. The Cat devoured the old Woman.

The Cat went along the road and perceived a Washerman with a donkey. He said, "O Cat, get away, or my donkey shall kick you to death!"

Thought the Cat, "I ate a basketful of cakes, I ate my friend the Parrot, I ate the abusive old Woman, and shall I blush to eat a Washerman?"

No, surely not. The Cat devoured the Washerman.

The Cat next met the wedding procession of a King: a column of soldiers, and a row of fine elephants two and two. The King said, "O Cat, get away, or my elephants will trample you to death."

Thought the Cat, "I ate a basketful of cakes, I ate my friend the Parrot, I ate the abusive old Woman, I ate the Washerman and his donkey, and shall I blush to eat a beggarly King?"

No, surely not. The Cat devoured the King, and his procession, and his elephants too.

Then the Cat went on until she met a pair of Landcrabs. "Run away, run away, Pussycat!" said the Landcrabs, "or we will nip you!"

"Ha! ha! ha!" laughed the Cat, shaking her sides (fat enough they were by this time), "I ate a basketful of cakes, I ate my friend the Parrot, I ate an abusive old Woman, I ate the Washerman and his donkey, I ate the King and all his elephants, and shall I run away from a Landcrab? Not so, but I will eat the Landcrab too!" So saying, she pounced upon the Landcrabs. Gobble, gobble, slip, slop: in two swallows the Landcrabs went down the Cat's gullet.

But although the Landcrabs slid down the Cat's gullet easily enough, you must know that they are hard creatures, too hard for a Cat to bite; so they took no harm at all. They found themselves amongst a crowd of creatures. There was the King, sitting with his head on his hands, very unhappy; there was the King's newly-wed bride in a dead faint; there was a company of soldiers, trying to form fours, but rather muddled in mind; there was a herd of elephants, trumpeting loudly; there was a donkey braying and the Washerman beating the donkey with a stick; there was the Parrot, whetting his beak on his own claws; then there was the old Woman abusing them all roundly; and last of all, five hundred cakes neatly piled in a corner. The Landcrabs ran round to see what they could find; and they found that the inside of the Cat was quite soft. They could not see anything at all, except by flashes, when the Cat opened her mouth, but they could feel. So they opened their claws, and nip! nip! nip!

"Miaw!" squealed the Cat.

Then came another nip, and another great Miaw!
The Landcrabs went on nipping, until they had nipped a big round hole in the side of the Cat. By this time the Cat was lying down, in great pain; and as the hole was very big, out walked the Landcrabs, and scuttled away.

Then out walked the King, carrying his bride; and out walked the elephants, two and two; out walked the soldiers, who had succeeded in forming fours-right, by your left, quick march! out walked the donkey, with the Washerman driving him along; out walked the old Woman, giving the Cat a piece of her mind; and last of all, out walked the Parrot, with a cake in each claw. Then they all went about their business, as if nothing had happened; and the Parrot flew back to whet his beak on the branch of the mango-tree.